Meet the Penguins!

Rory, Eddie & Clive

Looks: Rockhoppers have spiky yellow and black feathers on their heads that look like long eyebrows.

How big? 45 to 58 cm – about half the size of adult Emperor Penguins.

Favourite food: Shrimps.

Penguin party trick: Rockhopper Penguins love to burst from the water and land on the rocks with a belly flop.

Flipper fact: They hop from rock to rock, keeping both feet together and can jump up to one and a half meters.

Little Blue, Muriel, Hatty & Brenda

Looks: Fairy Penguins have blue feathers on their heads and backs but have white bellies.

How big? 30 to 33 cm – the world's smallest penguin.

Favourite food: Sardines and anchovies.

Penguin party trick: In the wild, Fairy Penguins are nocturnal so they only go on land at night (well past the Rockhoppers' bedtime).

Flipper fact: The world's smallest penguin – they are also known as the Little Penguin, or the Little Blue Penguin.

Paulie, Alaskadabra, Oo-Chi & Ku-Chi (chicks)

Looks: Emperor Penguins have black backs, white tummies and bright splashes of yellow and orange on their front and their ears. The chicks are fluffy and grey and their faces are white, not black.

How big?! Up to one meter tall – the world's tallest and heaviest penguin (over three times as tall as Little Blue!).

Favourite food: Squid.

Penguin party trick: When an egg is laid, the male stands with the egg on his feet to keep it warm until it hatches (this can take up to nine weeks).

Flipper fact: Emperor Penguins can stay under water for nearly twenty minutes!

Waldo, Warren and Wesley

Looks: Chinstrap Penguins get their name from the small black band that runs under their chin.

How big? Up to 68 cm (twice as tall as Fairy Penguins).

Favourite food: Little shrimps called krill.

Penguin party trick: Chinstraps are also known as Stonecracker Penguins because their call is so harsh it sounds like it could break stones.

Flipper fact: Chinstraps are the most common type of penguin – there are about thirteen million of them in the world.

Flighty Almighty

… Ahem, he's a GOOSE!

CHAPTER ONE

Where is Everybody?

There was a time when the greatest day out a kid could ever have was a trip to City Zoo. In the school holidays, the queue used to stretch from the ticket kiosk all the way down Royal Road as people flocked to see the pandas, the pythons and most of all,

the penguins.

But times had changed and nobody felt this more than Rory the rockhopper penguin. Since the day he hatched in the penguin enclosure he'd been the star attraction. Even as a chick, there was nothing he liked more than showing off his moves to the visitors.

Not so long ago, when Rory hopped on

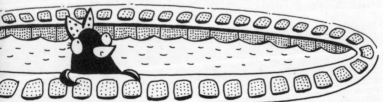

to the diving board and did his famous back flip with a triple somersault into the pool, the crowd went wild. They would cheer so loudly, you could hear them by the lion enclosure on the other side of the zoo. Today, there was silence.

"Where is everybody, Little Blue?" sighed Rory. "It was never this quiet when we were growing up, was it?"

His friend, the fairy penguin, tweaked his beak.

"That's because you were the one making all the noise, Rory... 'Let's have a cheeping competition, Blue. Let's throw our feeding dishes off the top diving board, Blue. Let's creep up on the bears and shout **"BOO!"** Blue!'"

Rory threw back his head and hooted.

"Fun, wasn't it?"

"The best," admitted Blue, grabbing hold of his tail. "Remember how I used to spin you round and round like this till you got dizzy and fell. The visitors loved that, didn't they?"

Suddenly she let go and Rory tottered across the ice, fell on his back and kicked his chubby legs in the air like a clown. But there was nobody there to laugh. Blue held out a flipper and helped him up.

"Why is no one coming to see us?" he wailed. "Is there a new baby panda stealing the show or something?"

"Maybe it's twin baby pandas," said Blue.

"Or maybe people have just gone off me," said Rory, hunching down next to her.

"Maybe my stunts suck and everyone's

gone to watch the oh-so-hilarious meerkats instead. What have meerkats got that I haven't got?"

Blue rolled her eyes.

"Let me think… Fur? A waistline? A sense of humour? Rory, get over yourself. It's early, loads of visitors will turn up at feeding time."

The two brown bears who lived in the paddock overlooking the penguin pool had been listening in to their conversation and interrupted.

"I wouldn't bet on it," said Orson. "The world of entertainment has moved on. No one wants to watch a bunch of birds eating fish heads any more."

"You're not even in colour. You're black and white," added Ursie.

It seemed that the bears were right. When Feeding Time arrived, apart from the zookeeper and his daughter, nobody else came to watch the penguins' antics. As Rory gulped down his ration of squid, he noticed that even Savannah seemed bored.

"Dad, I wanna go home," she said, texting madly on her mobile. "How come I have to hang out with you at the zoo every holiday? None of my friends hang out with their dads. It's soooo embarrassing."

The zookeeper wiped his hands on his overalls.

"I thought you loved the penguins."

Savannah stared at him hard from under her fringe.

"Yeah, like, when I was *two*. Penguins just stand there stinking of squid."

Rory almost choked. True, most of the penguins had fallen asleep on their feet after lunch but did they really stink? He had been Savannah's favourite since she was a toddler. Surely a little thing like how he smelled couldn't ruin their relationship? He tried to catch her eye, but Savannah tossed her hair and looked away.

"She didn't mean it," said Blue brightly. "She's a teenager. She's just trying to act cool."

But Rory wasn't convinced. He breathed heavily into Blue's face.

"Do I smell squiddy to you?"

She drew back and was just about to answer when the zookeeper turned to his daughter and made a sudden, shocking announcement.

"Well, you won't have to come to the zoo for much longer, love," he said. "The way things are going, it will have to shut down by the end of the season."

Shut the zoo? Rory's beak fell open in disbelief. He shook his head and told himself he'd got it wrong but Blue had heard it too. She was standing with her flippers over her ears, trying to block out the terrible news.

"Dad, you're joking, right?" said Savannah.

But the zookeeper was deadly serious.

"There aren't enough visitors. There isn't enough money coming in through the gates. Unless things pick up soon, we'll have to find new homes for all the animals, including my penguins."

Rory and Blue exchanged worried glances – if the zoo had to close, where would they live? City Zoo was the only home they had ever known. Savannah frowned and stopped texting.

"But Dad, they can't just close the zoo! They can't get rid of the penguins. I love them really. Rory is, like, my favourite person. Tell your boss he has to keep the penguins or I'll cry forever. If that doesn't work, tell him you need your job to pay for the new mobile you said I could have – the K135 is awesome."

The zookeeper picked up his empty fish bucket and sighed.

"It's not all about you, honey. Face facts, it costs a fortune to look after all the animals. If there isn't enough money, the penguins will have to go and I'll be out of work."

"But you have to do something!" wailed Savannah, running after him.

As soon as they'd gone, Rory and Blue began to panic.

"What if we end up in a zoo we hate?" wailed Rory. "What if they send us to another country? What if they send us to a wildlife reserve where things that eat penguins run wild?"

Blue held out her flippers in despair. "What if they split us up?"

Rory hadn't thought of that. Despite all

the teasing and tail-pulling, life without Blue was unthinkable and it seemed that she felt exactly the same about him. They waddled towards each other and went into a huddle, just like they used to when they were chicks.

"Are you scared?" whispered Blue.

"No," he mumbled, but she could feel his knees knocking.

"Are you lying, Rory?"

"I'm dancing."

Blue smiled sadly to herself and stood on his feet to keep them still. They clung to each other for comfort, then Rory broke away and punched the air.

"Penguin Power!" he shouted. "I'm not going without a fight, Blue. I have to think of a way to save this zoo!"

Chapter Two

Dangers of the Wild

"**H**ave you thought of a plan to save the zoo yet, Rory?" asked Blue, peering through his hutch window.

Rory yawned. He'd been awake all night trying to think of a way but so far, he'd come up with nothing.

"Of course I have a plan," he said. "It's brilliant."

"Yay!" whooped Blue. "I knew you would. What is it?"

"It's… very hard to describe," said Rory, hoping that an idea would magically come to him.

Blue tapped her small, pink foot impatiently.

"You don't have an idea, do you? I know when you're lying – your nostrils bubble."

Rory came out of his hutch wiping his beak.

"No, they don't… Oh, all right, I haven't come up with anything but it was impossible to think last night. All the animals were making such a noise."

"I didn't sleep either," admitted Blue.

By closing time the evening before, the news about the zoo shutting down had spread way beyond the penguin pool.

The bears told
the pigeon,

the pigeon told the squirrel,

and although the squirrel told the elephant not to breathe a word,

he was big enough to do whatever he pleased and immediately sounded his trumpet to alert the lions.

Once the lions got wind of it, the whole world knew. They roared so loudly, their relatives could hear them in deepest Africa. Through a relay of barks, squeaks, squawks and grunts, the word spread around the globe and by dawn, the whole of the animal kingdom from the smallest bug to the baleen whale knew about the fate of City Zoo.

By now, the penguins were very worried about where they might end up. There were tales spread by certain bears that there wouldn't be room in the other zoos for all of them and they would be taken abroad and released back into the wild.

Unfortunately, none of the penguins knew much about the countries their own species came from and their imaginations were running riot. Apart from their boss, Big Paulie the emperor penguin, they had all been bred in captivity. Blue's old enemy Muriel, who belonged to a girly gang of fairy penguins, was particularly upset.

"Oh my cod, I am *not* going to live in the wild!" she stamped. "I need my creature comforts. They're treating us like animals."

"What if they send me to Australia?" worried Blue. "Do koala bears eat penguins?"

"Yes, they do," insisted Muriel. "Penguins are their main diet. It'll be even worse for Rory though. He'll be sent to Chile to live with wild rockhoppers."

"What's so bad about Chile?" asked Rory.

"It's in the name, squidiot," she groaned. "It's called Chile because it's chilly. You'll freeze to death in seconds. You're not used to the climate."

She prodded the two anxious little penguins standing next to her.

"I'm right, aren't I, Brenda and Hatty? Chile is chilly. Not that Hatty would feel it through all her blubber."

Brenda and Hatty, who would rather be

eaten by koalas than shouted at by Muriel, nodded enthusiastically.

"Very chilly," said Hatty.

"Brrrrr," shivered Brenda.

Although the penguins were anxious at the idea of being left to fend for themselves in foreign parts, it didn't seem to bother Orson.

"Ah, stuff the zoo," he said. "So what if it closes? I'm sick of being cooped up on a fake mountain, day in, day out. Yee ha! I'm going back to Canada. I've got a cousin there. I'll call him on my new mobile when it arrives and tell him to make up the spare bed."

"You're getting a mobile?" scoffed Muriel. "Yeah right."

"I heard it with my own ears," said Ursie.

"Savannah said the K135 was for Orson."

Rory, who'd heard differently, felt it was only fair to put them straight.

"She said the K135 was *awesome*, not for Orson."

There was an embarrassed silence, punctuated with explosive tittering from Muriel, but Orson shrugged it off.

"So I won't phone Canada, I'll just turn up and say howdy. I can't wait! I'm going to run through the woods and catch wild salmon and…"

"I don't think so," said Ursie. "You run like an overstuffed teddy, you can't catch and salmon brings your bottom out in a rash. You wouldn't last five minutes in the Rockies."

Panic was breaking out all over the zoo

from the reptile house to the aquarium. The crocodile was scared he'd end up as a handbag if he was sent to Egypt, the spitting cobra's mouth went dry at the thought of being stuffed into a basket by an Indian snake charmer, the rhino was afraid he'd be poached in Africa, the camel was frightened he'd fry in Arabia and the warthog was so certain he'd be roasted wherever he went, he rolled in his own dung to make himself taste nasty.

When the zoo opened its gates later that morning, the few visitors who had bothered to come were very disappointed to find that most of the animals were not on display – they were hiding in fear of their lives.

The meerkats had gone underground, the leopard skulked into the back of his cave and even the hippo managed to disappear by holding his breath underwater. If he hadn't blown off like a thunderclap and given away his position with a string of bubbles no one would have known he was there.

"This zoo is rubbish!" cried a small boy. "I can't see any penguins!"

The penguins were there, but they were all hiding behind a fake cliff waiting for Big Paulie to lead them in a crisis meeting. For some reason, however, Big Paulie hadn't turned up. Every time the penguins had had a problem in the past, the mighty emperor penguin had sorted it. He'd been around for as long as anyone could remember.

He'd originally come from Antarctica and as he'd travelled by plane, he always joked that he was the only penguin capable of flight. If the stories were to be believed, Big Paulie was so tough, he could dive five hundred metres under the sea without his head exploding. He was so hard, he once trekked one hundred kilometres across the icy wastes without food. He was so brave, he'd rescued his own father from the jaws of a killer whale. No wonder the other penguins were a little scared of him.

"It's good that he's scary, Rory," Blue had once explained. "Remember the terrible Battle of Nesting Box between the rockhoppers and the chinstraps? If they'd had no respect for Paulie, they'd still be fighting over where to make their nests.

And what about the time he protected the emperor chicks from an escaped baboon? If it hadn't been scared of Paulie, it might have killed us all."

But time was ticking on, there was still no sign of Paulie and the penguins were getting impatient.

"It's unusual for him to be late," muttered Waldo, one of the chinstrap penguins. "Come to think of it, I haven't seen him for a while. I wonder if there's some sort of crisis?"

"Duh!" groaned Muriel. "There's a zoo-closing crisis. Does Paulie even know about it? If he won't come to us, we'll have to go to him, unless you ninnies have a better idea?"

"Rory has!" said Blue proudly. "He's thinking of a plan to save the zoo."

All the penguins shuffled round and stared at him hopefully.

"Let's hear it then," said Muriel, folding her flippers.

"Maybe later?" said Rory. "It still needs a little working on."

But Muriel wasn't prepared to wait.

"Here's my plan, *you* go and ask Paulie for help. Everybody get behind Rory!"

"You can go in front if you like," said Rory, but all the penguins formed an orderly line and waited for him to lead the way to Paulie's Palace. At this time of day, Big Paulie could usually be found working-out in his courtyard – he was famous for his one-flipper press-ups and had an amazing six-pack for a penguin – but when they got there, there was no sign of him.

"He's gone out," said Rory, relieved. "Let's come back tomorrow."

"Try knocking, bird-brain," said Muriel, rapping on the door. At the sound of footsteps, she pushed Rory forward. As the boss appeared, everyone else drew back, shocked by how scruffy Paulie looked.

His head feathers were sticking out like a punk rocker's and he smelled terrible.

"Eugh, what are those things stuck to his vest?" whispered Muriel. "Mouldy sequins?"

They were sprat eyes. Big Paulie, who was the best-groomed penguin in the zoo, had spilled fish down himself. It seemed he hadn't bothered to preen before hitting the nest and had fallen asleep in his day feathers. His eyes were bright red and though that was the natural colour for a rockhopper, emperor penguins had brown eyes. Maybe Paulie had been peeling onions – but where would he get them from? Whatever the cause, he wasn't himself at all.

"Tell Paulie the bad news, Rory," prompted Muriel.

Rory took a deep breath and was about to speak when Paulie held up a flipper for silence.

"I don't wanna know. I'm up to here with bad news."

He waved them away irritably and turned to go inside.

"Say something, Rory," urged Blue.

Rory plucked up all his courage.

"Paulie? This is serious. The zoo is going to close!"

One toe at a time, as if in great pain, Big Paulie shuffled round to face him again. Rory was expecting to be shouted at but Paulie just gazed at him glumly.

"So? Whadda you gonna do?"

"Me?" said Rory. "But you're the boss, Paulie. I... or rather, we... thought *you* might do something…"

Paulie stared into the distance as if he had nothing more to say, so Rory tried again.

"If they close this zoo, you might end up in a tiny tank in Sea World. Wouldn't that make you mad, Paulie?"

The boss made circles with his head as if he was trying to get rid of a wasp.

"Rory, Rory, whaddo I care? I'm mad with grief already. Yesterday, a migrating seagull told me that my best friend, Chubby O'Neil, was eaten by a leopard seal in the Arctic Ocean. That penguin was like a brother to me. The zoo shuts, whaddo I care? It won't bring Chubby back, may he rest in pieces."

He put his head under his wing. Rory

gulped and cleared his throat.

"Paulie, you have to help us! Penguins who have been friends for life will be separated forever, cast out into the wilderness to be eaten by fierce koalas…"

Paulie whipped his head out from under his wing.

"You dare to guilt-trip me about being separated from friends when my best friend Chubby is lost at sea for all eternity?"

"How could you, Rory," interrupted Muriel. "You are so insensitive."

But Paulie hadn't finished.

"You dare to lecture me about the dangers of the wild when Chubby just became a seal snack? I couldn't save him, I can't save you."

"C— could you at least try?" stammered Rory. "For… Chubby's sake?"

The mere mention of Chubby's name made Paulie wince and clutch at his heart.

"Cheap shot, Rory. Life ain't a bucket of caviar. Deal with it."

He kicked the door shut and the penguins scattered, apart from Muriel, who felt it was her moral duty to make Rory look like a loser in front of Blue.

"Well, you stuffed that up like a kipper," she smirked. "I can't wait to hear your 'amazing' plan to save the zoo – what was it again?"

"Just you wait and see!" said Rory with great bravado.

But he was bluffing. He still didn't have a plan, let alone an amazing one, and deep-down he was afraid that Muriel would have to wait rather a long time.

CHAPTER THREE

Penguin Cam-demonium

"**D**id I handle Paulie that badly?" sighed Rory as they waddled slowly back to the penguin pool. Blue shook her head.

"Take no notice of Muriel, she's all beak. You were brave and brilliant."

"I was, wasn't I?" he grinned, then he threw his flippers up in frustration. "But I *still* can't think of a way to save the zoo. Maybe it's because I've got a bird brain. I wish I was a great ape, they're almost as intelligent as humans."

"I heard more so," said Blue. "But it's not the size of your brain that counts, Rory. Little heads can have big thoughts. Let's go swimming. Maybe something will come to you in the deep end."

"Oh what, like a leopard seal?" said Rory sarcastically.

"I was only trying to help, squid breath!" said Blue. "Got a better idea?"

"Yes, we could go to the gift shop and buy mints," huffed Rory. "You're squiddy too, you know."

As they arrived at the pool, their argument was suddenly cut short. There was a strange metal object on a pole in the penguin enclosure and it was pointing straight at them.

"Duck!" hissed Rory.

"Chicken!" pouted Blue.

"No… *duck*! Keep your head down," whispered Rory, pulling her behind the nearest rock.

"It's a gun! They aren't going to release us into the wild, they're going to shoot us!"

For some while, the two of them huddled together quivering, waiting for the bullets to start. They might have stayed there all day if Muriel hadn't wandered over with Hatty and Brenda and got the wrong idea.

"Ooh, look girls!" she sang. "Ro-ry and Bloopy sitting in a tree, K. I. S. S. I. N. G.!

It's not even breeding season."

"We are *not* sitting in a tree!" insisted Rory. "Get down before they blow your heads off."

Muriel preened herself and didn't move.

"Oh my cod, he's been drinking seawater," she sneered. "He's gone crazy."

She looked down her beak at Rory.

"Bloop, why are you even hanging out with a boy?"

"I'm not 'hanging out'," said Blue. "I just don't want to be shot by that gun."

Muriel, Hatty and Brenda threw up their flippers and cackled.

"What's so funny?" said Rory.

"It's not a gun, dummy. It's a camera," said Muriel, posing in front of it. "Smile, we're on Penguin Cam. Preen yourself,

Bloop, you look like you lost in a pillow fight."

"How do you know it's a camera?" said Rory.

Muriel looked at him as if he was completely thick.

"Radio Brown Bear, Orson and Ursie, told us. They heard the zookeeper talking to Savannah about it while we were all watching you screw things up at Paulie's."

Rory stood up and stared at the weird contraption overhanging the enclosure. Now that he'd studied it properly, he could see that it had a lens similar to the ones visitors used to point at him when he was doing stunts. He scratched his head with his foot and tried to make sense of it.

"*Penguin* Cam? What on earth is that?

43

What does it do?" wondered Blue out loud. Muriel stopped posing with Hatty and Brenda and pulled a face.

"Oh my cod, she doesn't even know what Penguin Cam is," she snickered. "You really need to get with the programme, Bloop."

Blue screwed up her beak and glared at her.

"My name is not *Bloop*!"

"Oooh! Don't get your flippers in a flap!" snorted Muriel. "Actually, do! Every little tantrum you throw will be captured on Penguin Cam and watched by millions of people on the internet. They're watching you right now."

Blue had no idea what the internet was and whisked round nervously.

"I can't see anyone."

"No, but they can see you-hoo. Come along, Hatty and Brenda. It's time for your makeovers. I can't be seen with ugly friends worldwide."

Blue watched them go and, confused and frightened, she put her face in her flippers to hide it from the camera.

"I don't like it looking at me, Rory. I don't want millions of people to catch us in a net like Muriel said."

Rory tried to think of something helpful to say, but he knew a lot more about trout than technology.

"I don't think that's *quite* what Muriel said, and anyway, she often tells lies, Blue."

It was no comfort at all and Blue could only think the worst.

"Maybe the internet is like a fishing

net," she wailed. "Instead of shooting us, they're going to catch us in a giant net and put us on a plane to Australia and Chile!"

Rory put his flippers on her shoulders and tried to calm her down.

"They won't, it wouldn't make any sense," he said. "There must be easier ways to catch penguins, like rounding us up with dogs…"

"You're not helping!" squeaked Blue.

Rory backed off.

"OK, OK. I bet the bears have got it wrong, just like they did with the mobile. I'll go and see them and find out."

He was certain the whole business about the net was a load of nonsense, but having woken the bears who were sleeping under the tree that overhung the enclosure, it seemed that Orson and Ursie had got it almost right.

"We got it straight from the zookeeper's mouth," said Orson. "He was talking to his daughter about setting the video camera up so people could watch the goings-on in the penguin pool all day on their pooters and top-laps."

"But why would they want to?" said Rory. "Nothing goes on. OK, I do a few tricks but mostly, we eat, we poop, we sleep."

"It was Savannah's idea," insisted Orson. "It's been tried at another zoo with chimps and she saw them picking their noses and things on the internet. Apparently, Chimp Cam was so hilarious, people wanted to see the animals for real. The number of visitors doubled and made the zoo a whole heap of money."

"So Savannah told her dad," continued Ursie, "and the zookeeper set up a camera to film your hilarious capers in the hope that it'll bring more visitors here. There's only one thing I don't understand…"

"What's that?" asked Rory.

"Why have Penguin Cam when they could have Bear Cam? We're much more entertaining. Orson, give me your paw!"

Ursie grabbed hold of Orson and they went into a tap dance routine using an old umbrella that had blown into the bear pit.

"Hollywood, here we come!" said Ursie. "We do this all the time when no one's looking, don't we, Orson? Anything to ease the boredom."

Rory watched them and as he watched, he had a brilliant idea – it was staring him right in the face. He raced back to Blue.

"Listen, the net thing is brilliant. It's made me think of a way to save the zoo! If we want to attract visitors back through Penguin Cam, all we need to do is put on the greatest show on earth!"

"All?" said Blue. "We? Who? How?"

Rory paced up and down excitedly as the plan grew in his head.

"Whatever we do, it has got to be better than chimps weeing or bears scratching," he said, thinking out loud. "I've got it! I'll get a penguin stunt team together! We can do high dives, snowboarding, toboggan racing, acrobatics…"

Blue punched the air.

"Yay! People will love it. Visitors will come flocking. I knew you'd think of something... where are you going now?"

"I'm off to find Eddie and Clive," he said. "We need to start training – see you!"

With that, Rory skidded off to find his two best friends who weren't girls and left Blue standing there all on her own.

CHAPTER FOUR

The Greatest Show on Earth

Although Blue was delighted that Rory had thought of a wonderful plan to save the zoo, she couldn't understand why he hadn't come back to talk to her about it. He'd been gone for ages. How long did it take to ask his mates if they wanted to be in the stunt team?

She had ideas for some spectacular stunts which she wanted to share and she was keen to start training. She went to look for Rory.

He was practising a snowboard stunt between two rocks with his mates, Eddie and Clive.

He usually ignored Blue when he was with them. They had made it very clear that it wasn't cool to talk to girl penguins – even though Eddie secretly fancied Hatty and Clive secretly fancied Brenda.

Being ignored by her best friend hurt a little, but Blue understood that Rory didn't mean to be mean. It was just a boy thing. But surely he was grown up enough to rise above it for the sake of the greatest show on earth? She watched the three of them for a while, waiting for Rory to ask her to join in.

When he didn't, she broke the rules and waved at him in front of his friends. He muttered something to Eddie and Clive who looked at Blue irritably and sloped off. Once they'd gone, Rory ambled over to see her and was surprised to find there was a bit of an atmosphere.

"Did you see what I was doing with Eddie and Clive there, great stunt, eh? Those boys are good. We're going to nail this... What's up, Blue?"

Blue pretended she was fine – she didn't want him to think she was a silly, sulky, girly penguin like Muriel.

"Nothing's up. Hey, I've got some ideas for our stunt team, want to hear them? I could do that thing when I flip my snowboard three times, only I could do it off that high rock and..."

"You?" said Rory.

"Of course me," said Blue. "Yeah, yeah, I know it's dangerous but so what if it keeps people watching on Penguin Cam... Why

55

are you looking at me like that, Rory?"

"It's an all-boys team," he mumbled.

Blue looked at him in disbelief.

"But I can snowboard faster than Eddie! And I can dive deeper than Clive! That's not fair!"

Rory knew she was right. No one could stay under water longer than Blue, apart from Big Paulie. She was so light, he could lift her up to perform the most daring stunts. He really wanted her in the team but would he ever live it down if he asked his mates to let a girl penguin in on their act?

"You might get hurt, Blue."

"Like that's the reason!" she snapped. "I'm not stupid, this is about Eddie and Clive. You care more about looking cool in front of them than looking brilliant in front of the camera, you big wet jellyfish!"

Stunned by her outburst, Rory decided he'd rather stand up to his mates and persuade them that girls were OK than face such an angry, disappointed Blue.

"I'll talk to them," he said. "Just don't go all Muriel on me."

As he skated away, Blue shouted after him.

"Oi... Jellyfish? Don't you *ever* call me Muriel!"

After she'd calmed down a bit, she decided to practise her tobogganing techniques in case Eddie and Clive needed more convincing that she was as good as them. She hopped right up to the top of the very high, very long curved ramp that was built over the penguin pool, waved to Penguin Cam and lay down on her belly. Taking a deep breath, she pushed off against the wall as hard as she could with both feet and shot forward.

The ramp was a lot more slippery than she had expected and as Blue gathered speed and hurtled down faster and faster, she was forced to close her eyes – which is why she didn't see Muriel bending over at the bottom of the ramp preening her tail feathers.

Muriel didn't see Blue either and the next thing she knew, she'd been hit at thirty miles an hour by a speeding fairy penguin and went bum over beak into the water. It sounded as if a walrus had jumped into the pool from a helicopter and the other penguins came hurrying over to see what all the shouting was about.

"What happened, dear?" called Waldo the chinstrap penguin, peering into the water. "Did you trip over your own tongue?"

"OH MY COD, she pushed me!" screamed Muriel as she came up for air, pointing angrily at Blue. "What is your *problem?*"

Blue tried her best to apologise.

"I'm really sorry, Muriel. I didn't see you there. I just wanted to prove I was good enough to be in the stunt team."

"What stunt team?" muttered Muriel from under her soggy fringe.

"Mine," said a voice behind her.

It was Rory. Standing beside him were Eddie and Clive. He'd persuaded them to let Blue be in the team by bribing them with a mackerel each and he'd come to tell her the good news. As Hatty and Brenda hauled Muriel out of the water, she looked at the line-up and snorted.

"*This* is your dream team? Dopey, Tubby, Mad and Clumsy? Good luck with that."

"It's for a good cause," said Rory.

"Is it?" said Eddie, who wasn't the smartest penguin in the pool.

"We're doing it to save the zoo," explained Rory. "If we perform some really good stunts on Penguin Cam, people are bound to want to come and see us for real."

The cluster of penguins who had gathered around Rory thought it was a great idea... all except for Muriel.

"No one's going to want to watch *you*," she said.

"Why not?" asked Rory, doing a back flip with a head spin to prove his point.

Muriel gathered her girls around her.

"Because they will be too busy watching *us*," she said. "I had the same idea as you did yesterday, only my idea is better... isn't that right, Hatty?"

"You did? Oh yes, much better idea. We're a stunt team, right?"

"We're a synchronised swimming team," said Muriel, kicking her ankle away. "You remember don't you, Brenda?"

"Yes – don't slap me!" mumbled Brenda.

"See?" said Muriel. "Forget your silly stunt team, Rory. That won't 'Save The Zoo'. People want to see a bit of glamour, not a load of podgy penguins skidding down a slide. Come along, girls, we need to practise. Bloop, you're in my team."

"But I'm in the stunt team," said Blue, appealing to Eddie and Clive. "Aren't I?"

They shuffled about, avoiding her gaze.

"I think we can take that as a no," smirked Muriel, who didn't see Rory mouthing, *Two mackerels each*, to his friends.

"It's a yes," said Clive. "Blue is in our team."

"I like mackerel!" beamed Eddie.

Blue flung her flippers around both

of them but Clive, who had never been hugged by a girl penguin before, froze to the spot.

"Let's keep it professional, shall we?" he squeaked. "Or I'll change my mind."

"I like it!" said Eddie. "Hug me harder."

Muriel waved her flippers madly.

"Do you boys seriously want Bloop in your team? She can't even slide down the ramp without causing an accident."

"Yes they do," said Rory.

"Yes we do!" agreed Eddie. "Can I have three mackerels now, Rory?"

Muriel looked Blue up and down and put her beak in the air.

"Oh well, break an egg, as they say in showbiz."

"All right, Muriel. You do your thing.

We'll do ours," said Rory, trying to keep the peace. "Let's just try not to tread on each other's toes, OK?"

But it was not OK with Muriel, and now that he'd put the idea into her head, she was determined to tread on as many toes as possible.

Chapter Five

Bird Fight

Muriel wasn't happy and when Muriel wasn't happy, everybody knew about it.

She'd spent the best part of the afternoon working out a brilliant routine for her synchronised swimming team, but in practice, it just wasn't working.

Despite the fact that penguins are very good swimmers, certain fairy penguins wouldn't do as they were told. Hatty and Brenda couldn't seem to grasp even the most basic moves and were bobbing up and down in the middle of the pool like bolshy babies.

"Scull, girls! Scull!" screamed Muriel, who was standing on a rock demonstrating the movement impatiently with her flippers.

"Schoolgirls?" mumbled Hatty. "Did she say schoolgirls, Brenda? I can't hear, I've got water in my ears."

"I think she said seagulls," shrugged Brenda.

Muriel had a horrible feeling that her perfect piece of choreography was dead in the water.

"What is the *matter* with you two?" she groaned. "I've seen ostriches swim better. Do you really want Rory's stupid stunt team to look cooler than us on Penguin Cam?"

Hatty and Brenda shook their heads miserably.

"Well, that's what's going to happen," she said, "unless you do as I say. Right, let's go over it again and this time, concentrate. Watch me and learn!"

Muriel dived into the pool and demonstrated the main positions again.

"This is Front Layout," she called, floating face down. Hatty and Brenda took deep breaths and copied her. By then, Muriel had flipped on to her back and was cruising plumply around the pool with her beak in the air.

"This is Back Layout… are you with me, girls?"

She looked over her shoulder to make sure they were doing it properly but to her extreme annoyance, both penguins were still floating on their fronts as they hadn't heard her instructions. Muriel dived under the water and gnashed her beak at them.

"Keep up! Front layout! Back layout! Go straight into ballet legs... and lift!" she commanded, raising her chubby knees high out of the water like a prima ballerina.

"I'm drowning!" gurgled Hatty.

"Don't fuss. Point your toes!" shouted Muriel. "And scull... and scull... and scull..."

As Hatty and Brenda floundered in the deep end, it became clear to Muriel that they were going to need an awful lot more practice if they were going to be better than the boys.

"Right, let's do it all over again!" she insisted, treading water furiously. "I'm going to throw in a new element and when I say 'throw', that's exactly what I mean."

The rest of the team exchanged worried

glances as she explained.

"Keep with the beat," said Muriel. "On the day we'll have real music but for now, I'll go *la la la* and on the count of three, we'll throw you in the air, Brenda."

"*Why?*" wailed Brenda. "Why would you *do* that to me?"

"So you can perform a pirouette and land on our shoulders, and because you're not as heavy as Fatty. I mean Hatty," said Muriel. "The kids will love it. You'll be a knock-out."

But as Team Muriel counted to three and flung Brenda up into the air, she slipped, booted Hatty in the head and knocked her out cold.

"Oh, great!" snapped Muriel as Hatty recovered on the side of the pool. "One of you is too lardy to lift and the other has brain damage. My creative genius is wasted!"

"Sorry, Muriel," squeaked Brenda.

"Morry, Suriel," spluttered Hatty, who was still a bit concussed.

"You will be when the zoo shuts forever," she muttered.

"Maybe if I eat less squid, I'll be light enough to throw," said Brenda hopefully.

"Like that's ever going to happen," snorted Muriel. "No, what we need is a tiny penguin with a lot of guts and less blubber…" She threw back her beak and smiled. "…And I know *exactly* where to find her!"

Leaving strict instructions for Hatty and Brenda to practise their egg-beater kicks until their thighs were numb, Muriel waddled over to spy on Team Rory. Hiding

behind Paulie's Palace, she watched with
mounting jealousy as they plummeted
down the waterslide, flipped and formed a
penguin pyramid on the artificial glacier.

Seeing Blue balanced on top as sweetly as a cherry on a cupcake was more than Muriel could bear.

With a mad shriek, she threw herself on to her stomach and scooted towards them across the ice. As Rory watched in horror, she stuck her head up her stubby tail, curled into a ball and bowled straight into Clive and Eddie. As their knees buckled, the pyramid wobbled and collapsed in a squealing heap with Blue underneath.

"Whoops," said Muriel, preening herself.

Luckily, the penguins were well padded and nobody was hurt, but their pride had been badly dented. Rory brushed himself down angrily.

"Why would you do that, Muriel?"

She shrugged and carried on preening.

"It's i…cy? I slipped."

Rory saw red. "You did that on purpose, you… you… slimy sea slug!"

Muriel put her head on one side. "Did I really? And what are you going to do about it?"

For a moment, Rory did nothing. He was too much of a gentleman to hit a lady penguin, but Muriel was no lady. He couldn't let her get away with humiliating his team like this. Fixing her with what he hoped was a menacing stare, he squared up to her.

"Go on, Rory, beak her flippers!" yelled Clive.

"Go on, Rory, flip her beakers!" yelled Eddie.

The commotion soon attracted the

brown bears who were keen to grab a ringside seat.

"Come quickly, Orson… Bird Fight!" shouted Ursie.

Blue jumped up and down beside Rory.

"Don't lower yourself to Muriel's level!" she cried.

"Oh, please do!" insisted Ursie. "We haven't been to a good fight since the gorilla got his keeper in a headlock."

Rory raised his flippers.

"What are you going to do, squid-for-brains?" teased Muriel. "Slap me?"

Rory couldn't hold back. He grabbed hold of Muriel's perfectly groomed head and, using both flippers, he ruffled her precious plumage so hard, it went static.

"No!" shrieked Muriel. "Anything but the ruffling. Get off, I've just preened!"

But encouraged by the bears, Rory couldn't stop and by the time he'd finished, Muriel looked like a feather duster attacked by a rabid dog. For a moment, she stood there fuming and unable to accept defeat, then she darted forward and pecked Rory on the shoulder. A drop of blood fell on to the ice and there was a gasp from the bears.

"Woah… pecking's below the belt, lady!" roared Orson. "Stop the fight."

"Nobody wants to see that on Penguin Cam," added Ursie. "Do you really think parents are going to pay to bring their kiddiwinks here to see you two draw blood?"

Team Rory and the bears looked at Muriel in disgust, then Ursie started tutting. Muriel hated it when Ursie tutted.

"*What?*" she wailed. "Why are you all staring at me? I didn't mean to peck you, Rory. I didn't even do it hard. You must have over-sensitive skin."

"Just go, Muriel," he said.

As Muriel swept off in a huff, Rory told Eddie and Clive he'd catch them later and disappeared behind a rock. He clearly wanted to be alone, but Blue followed him.

"Does your shoulder hurt, Rory?"

She touched the wound where the feathers were stained a little pink and he turned away.

"Don't fuss, I'm not a fledgling."

Blue flicked his beak.

"Someone got out of his nest the wrong side today."

Rory flicked her back and sighed.

"Ursie's right. No one wants to see penguins fight. But as long as Muriel's around, that's what's going to happen."

Blue sighed and watched as a group of chinstrap penguins gathered nearby. As they began to play their own version of hopscotch with a round pebble and sticks, a thought suddenly struck her.

"Penguin Cam shouldn't be about rockhoppers v fairy penguins, Rory. Why have two acts when we could have lots? People like variety. We could put on a talent show!"

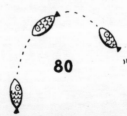

The more she thought about it and the more he thought about it, the bigger the idea grew.

"The chinstraps are very artistic and theatrical. Maybe Waldo could put on a play with those two arty friends of his."

"You mean Wesley and Warren?" said Rory. "They'd be good. They make me laugh even when they're not doing anything."

"The rockhopper girls could disco dance," said Blue, "or perform a classic ballet like *Penguin Lake*, and the emperor chicks could ice skate – they'd look really cute. Oh, and how about a magic act?"

Rory jumped up and spun round – this could be just what the zoo needed.

"The more acts, the merrier! Let's go

and tell everyone about the show, Blue. I'll tell the boys, you tell the girls."

There was just one problem – who was going to tell Muriel?

CHAPTER SIX

Chicks and Chinstraps

"**W**e'd better tell Muriel about the talent show before we tell the others," said Blue. "If she's the last to hear, she'll never go along with it."

Rory didn't care if he never spoke to Muriel again, but if they didn't come to some sort of agreement, she could ruin the whole show out of spite. She was probably plotting to get him back right now, as payback for the ruffling.

"It will be better coming from you, Blue," he said. "It was your idea and you're good at explaining things."

Blue looked at him sideways.

"You're scared of her, aren't you?"

"I'd rather swim with sharks," admitted Rory.

They decided to tell Muriel together and waddled over to the other side of the pool.

There was no sign of the enemy, but according to Waldo, she was having her feathers washed and set by Brenda, at Hutch Number 12.

"We'd better not disturb her," said Rory.

"Yes, we had," said Blue, knocking fearlessly on the door. "Muriel, can we squark?"

Brenda came to the window.

"Muriel says to tell you she doesn't want to squeak to you again."

"Never!" screeched Muriel.

Rory turned to go. "Let's try later when she's in a better mood."

"That could be years," said Blue. "Brenda, can you give Muriel a message, please? Can you tell her that instead of just doing two acts on Penguin Cam there's going to be a great big talent show…"

Before she finished explaining, Muriel appeared, one half of her head perfectly smooth and the other half still ridiculously ruffled.

"What talent show? Whose idea was this?"

Blue and Rory pointed at each other nervously.

"His… hers… ours."

"No, it was *my* idea," said Muriel. "I thought of it ages ago while I was having my feathers straightened, didn't I, Brenda?"

Brenda looked rather confused until Muriel poked her in the eye.

"Brenda, didn't I say it would be better to have a talent show with lots of acts instead of Rory's stupid one?"

"Oh yes, and ours," blundered Brenda.

Blue was annoyed that her idea had been hijacked but she swallowed her pride, even though it stuck in her throat like a fishbone. Muriel was up for it, that was all that mattered, so Blue tried to make peace with her.

"I've heard your act is brilliant, Muriel," she lied. "The bears said so."

"It will be even better when you're in it," said Muriel. "We need a flyer, someone skinny we can throw in the air. We're rehearsing in five minutes. Chop, chop!"

Blue looked at her agog.

"But you know I'm in Rory's team."

"Not any more," said Muriel. "I'm a penguin short and you're a short penguin. You're either with Team Muriel or there will be no talent show – even if it was my idea. Fetch my diary, Brenda, I need to hold auditions for my show."

"It's not your show," insisted Rory. "It's everybody's. Anyone can take part. They don't have to audition."

Muriel flicked through her diary.

"Yes they do. I don't want any more rubbish acts in my show. I'm already stuck with yours… I have a window at six o'clock tomorrow for the auditions, we'll hold them then. Run along now. No, not you, Bloop. Brenda needs to teach you our routine."

Muriel had put her big webbed foot down and although Rory argued that losing a team member had cost him four mackerel, Blue knew she had no choice but to go with Muriel for the sake of all the penguins.

"You'll need a beak peg for synchronised swimming, Bloop," said Muriel triumphantly. "What size is that conk of yours, extra large? Or does it just look that way because your head is like a ping pong ball?"

With an apologetic wave, Rory left Blue to the mercy of Muriel and wandered off to spread the word about the talent show on his own. He wasn't sure how keen the other penguins would be, but nobody could have been more enthusiastic than the two emperor chicks who were huddled together fatly after the sardine supper their mothers regurgitated for them.

"Oooh yeth!" they lisped. "Uth wanth to be in it."

"The auditions will be at six o'clock tomorrow after closing time," explained Rory.

Hearing that it would be way past their bedtime, they were even more excited.

"Ooh! After our bye-bythe? Uth can thtay up late like big penguinth!"

"Me ith going to win cute-etht chick!" said Oo-Chi.

"No, you ithn't, me is. *Me* ith cute-etht, me win!" said Ku-Chi.

Rory was beginning to wonder if asking them to take part was such a good idea after all. Being cute was all very well but it would hardly be exciting to watch unless the chicks actually got up and did something.

"Can you ice skate?" he asked.

"Thkate?" said Oo-Chi. "Of courth we can, thilly."

"Yeth," said Ku-Chi. "We can thkate on ithe, we can thkate on wockth…"

"We can thkate in the cloudth up in the thky…" said his sister.

Now who's being silly, thought Rory but they were only babies, so he played along with it.

"You can be Chicks On Ice. See you at the auditions, six o'clock tomorrow, don't be late."

Oo-Chi looked at Rory with her head on one side.

"Excuthe me, Wory... when ith tomorrow?"

Rory's heart sank. If the chicks couldn't tell the time, what were the chances of them turning up at all?

"Tomorrow is the day after today," he said patiently.

"No, it ithn't! That'th yethderday," argued Ku-Chi. "Wory? When ith thixth o'clock?"

"Anyone knowth that!" said his sister. "It'th when the big hand ith on theven and the lickle hand ith on eleventy!"

"Ask your mums to bring you," sighed Rory.

It was a relief to talk to the chinstraps. They were a bit odd but they were charming and keen and when Rory asked what talents they had, they suggested some very interesting ideas.

"Well, sporting events are out, love," said Waldo. "We're highly creative but we're not what you'd call athletic."

"Not like you," said Warren, twirling the handsome moustache he was wearing. He'd made it from a wig that one of the elephants had snatched from its keeper. He'd stuck it on with a bit of bubble gum and it gave him an individual look, to say the least.

"We're artists," said Wesley, proudly.

Rory tried to look impressed. He was looking for different acts, but he wasn't quite sure what they could bring to the show apart from false facial hair.

"Culture, dear boy," said Waldo.

"We will create a tableau on the rocks," said Warren. "A three-dimensional piece of artwork made from rubbish which we shall rearrange into a thing of great beauty and worth."

Rory had no idea what they were talking about, but then he didn't know much about art.

"Will it look good on Penguin Cam?" he asked.

"It will look divine," said Warren.

"Sublime," agreed Wesley. "It will all become clear at the audition – see you there!"

Rory had his doubts, but maybe people would enjoy it. He was just on his way to ask the rockhopper girls to come up with a dance routine when he bumped into Eddie and Clive practising a new stunt on their snowboards.

"Hey, Rory, I know a secret," said Eddie. "There's going to be a talent show with lots of different acts – not just ours."

"You don't say?" smiled Rory.

"The bears told us. They said it was their idea. Does this change anything?" asked Clive. "Are we still doing our snowstunts and stuff?"

"You betcha," said Rory. "Only I'm afraid we've lost Blue."

Eddie pulled his sad face. "Oh, man! I'm sor-ree. Was she eaten by a leopard seal like Flabby O'Neil?"

Clive rolled his eyes.

"We just saw her, Eddie, remember? Blue was in the pool and Muriel was giving her a really hard time."

Eddie clutched his own beak. "Ooh yeah. I wouldn't want Muriel to snap a peg on me like that."

Rory was already feeling guilty about letting Muriel take Blue and now he felt a whole lot worse. "I'm going over there," he said.

"But we need to practise our act," said Clive.

"We can't be Team Rory without a Rory," added Eddie.

"I'll find time," said Rory. "As soon as I've made sure Blue is OK and spoken to the rockhopper girls, I'll come and find you."

But he didn't, because on the way he went past Paulie's Palace, saw him gazing mournfully out of the open window, and in a foolish, crazy, overexcited moment, Rory leaned in and asked him to take part in the auditions.

"I thought maybe you could sing something," he said brightly. "You emperors have the best voices."

It was amazing how speedily Paulie's expression switched from sorrow to rage.

"Whadda you, nuts?" he bellowed. "You

think I'm in the mood for singing when my soul mate Chubby O'Neil has sung his last song?"

"I just thought it might take your mind off it," cringed Rory. "And h— help the zoo?"

Paulie beckoned menacingly with the tip of his flipper.

"I don't think you heard me the first time or you wouldn't be here."

Rory was shaking so hard, he could hardly waddle but Paulie kept beckoning until their bellies touched, then he breathed in his ear.

"If you bother me again on this matter, I'll have you thrown to my good friend Mr Tiger."

"I'll be off then," squeaked Rory.

Two talentless chicks, three mad artists and no singer. Not much of a line-up, thought Rory. But if Big Paulie and Mr Tiger got their way, it wasn't just the talent show that was going down with a whimper.

CHAPTER SEVEN

Rory Gets Goosed

After the zoo had closed the following evening, Rory and Muriel got ready to hold the auditions. After a great deal of argument, it had been agreed that they should both judge the acts. Although none of the other penguins had voted for

Muriel, she voted for herself several times and cheated her way on to the panel.

It was a shame, because no matter how good or bad the acts were, Muriel seemed determined to make fishpaste out of them. The first to come up against her was an elderly emperor penguin who introduced himself as Alaskadabra.

"That's a stupid name," she said. "What are you going to do for us?"

The penguin shuffled about nervously, took out a bendy drinking straw he'd found in the pool and waved it around like a wand.

"I'm a magician."

"I'll be the judge of that," said Muriel. "Go on then, work your magic."

Alaskadabra smiled shyly and began

to pull a string of silk hankies out of the pouch under his belly but somehow, one of the knots got caught under his tail and, giving the string a hard yank, he flipped himself over like a pancake and landed in an undignified heap.

While the audience of invited penguins and uninvited bears thought it was hilarious, Muriel was not amused.

"Haven't you got anything else up your sleeve?" she muttered. "Can you make yourself disappear?"

Alaskadabra cupped his ear hole with his flipper.

"Beg pardon? I'm a little hard of hearing."

"Make yourself disappear!" bellowed Muriel.

To her surprise, he took her at her

word, bowed apologetically and sloped off. Muriel tutted and turned to Rory.

"Where's he going? He hasn't done a single trick yet. What a time waster!"

Rory's webbed toes curled in frustration. "Muriel, please try and be more positive about the acts," he whispered. Chicks On Ice were arriving and they looked so eager, the last thing he wanted was for her to upset them.

"Be more positive?" simpered Muriel. "OK. These two look positively ridiculous."

The chicks teetered about on the ice holding flippers as they faced the judges.

"What are your names?" asked Rory gently.

Overcome with shyness, the chicks put their heads under their wings.

"We're not thaying," murmured Oo-Chi.

"We're a bit thcared," squeaked Ku-Chi.

"Come on, I haven't got all day," barked Muriel. "Either grow up or get off!"

The chicks peered at her in horror then flumped down and cheeped loudly for their mothers, who came and dragged them off, cursing Muriel as they left.

"Typical pushy parents," said Muriel. "This is a talent show, ladies. Not a nursery."

Just when Rory thought things couldn't get any worse, the next act came on.

"I'll handle this one, Muriel," said Rory, boldly. "If you upset anyone else, we'll have nobody to put through."

He smiled encouragingly at the

contestant standing in front of him and asked his name.

"I am Flighty Almighty," he replied. "Unlike any penguin known to man or beast, I can fly through the air with the greatest of ease! I can flip, I can flap..."

"You can flop," muttered Muriel as Flighty hopped up the steep artificial cliff and waddled on to the top diving board.

"Give him a chance," insisted Rory.

Flighty teetered to the edge of the diving board, clung on with his toes then went into freefall.

"Boo!" yelled Orson. "That's not flying, that's falling. Any old fool can do that!"

"Look at me, I'm 'flying'," heckled Ursie, falling headfirst off a log.

Then, just as Flighty Almighty was about

to hit the water, he spread out his flippers
and to everyone's amazement he swooped
up, soared into the sky and circled above
their heads.

"Oooooooh!" gasped Hatty.

"Ahhhhhh!" cheered Brenda.

"Shhhhhhh!" hissed Muriel. "So he can linger in the air, so can bad smells."

But Rory was beside himself with excitement. This was the act that could save the zoo! Visitors would come from far and wide to see the world's only flying penguin.

"What did I tell you, Muriel?" he beamed. "That guy's got something really different about him."

"That penguin's got a very funny beak, hasn't he, Clive?" said Eddie at the top of his voice as Flighty Almighty did another circuit. "It almost looks as if it's been stuck on."

Clive tried to shush him, but as the amazing flying penguin skimmed the water with his flipper and did a victory roll, Eddie piped up again.

"He's got funny flippers too, hasn't he,

Clive? Almost like they don't belong to him."

"Never judge a penguin by its cover," hissed Clive. "Now shush."

As Flighty Almighty made a perfect landing in front of the judges, the audience clapped and cheered.

"Wow!" said Rory. "You are 160 per cent the best act we've seen all evening."

Even Muriel had to admit it was a terrific performance and was about to put Flighty through to the show when Orson butted in.

"That guy cheated!"

"Yes," added Ursie. "Not much gets past us. He's the wrong species."

Realising he'd been caught in the act, Flighty tried to creep off, but it was too late. Muriel had already noticed the black paint dripping off his wings, which he'd cunningly disguised as flippers. She marched over and twanged his false beak.

"Oh, well-judged, Rory. You said he was different and you were right. He's not a penguin, he's a *goose*!"

There was a collective gasp from the penguins in the audience. Rory rubbed his eyes but no matter how he looked at it, the creature standing before him was definitely a goose.

"So? I do impressions," protested Flighty. "Give me a break."

"Sorry," sighed Rory. "It's against the rules. If it was Goose Cam maybe."

"You're disqualified!" said Muriel.

The goose honked loudly, flapped off

and the bears started heckling the judges.

"Never had you down as a goosist, Rory!" yelled Orson.

"You'll be ostracising the ostriches next," added Ursie. "You'll be calling the Lyre Birds liars."

"Oh, that's a good one!" crowed Orson.

It was pointless trying to defend himself once the bears had started to play with words. By now, Rory felt like forgetting the whole thing and going back to his nest, but he had to get his acts together. The show had to go on.

"Why so glum, dear boy?" said Waldo. He had just arrived with Warren and Wesley who were struggling under the weight of various items that had been thrown into the penguin enclosure over the years, including a lampshade which Warren was wearing on his head.

"Are the dustmen on strike?" shouted Orson.

"What a load of old rubbish," grumbled Ursie.

Waldo cleared his throat and waved a kettle in the air.

"We are the Arty Party Penguins and we will now turn these unlovely, unwanted items into an image of beauty."

"Great," said Rory generously. "Ready when you are."

The three penguins took a deep bow, then, waddling off with the rubbish, they rearranged it carefully between them on the grass. It took some time and even Rory was beginning to lose the will to live. Just

as he'd almost nodded off, the Arty Party Penguins threw up their flippers in unison and cried,

"Ta… Da!"

"Ta da?" said Rory as kindly as he could. "What's it meant to be?"

"Well, if you knew the first thing about art, it's obvious," said Waldo waspishly.

"It's as plain as the beak on your face," said Warren, adjusting his moustache.

"It's a 3D image of Her Majesty the Queen," said Wesley.

Rory had never seen the Queen but even so, he doubted she wore a kettle on her head. The artwork didn't bear much likeness to anything, let alone anybody as far as he could see.

"You have to stand in a certain way,"

said Waldo, "and view it from above."

"It's obvious, Rory," said Muriel who had an enormous crush on Warren and his moustache. "I've met the Queen, you haven't, that's what she looks like. Don't argue."

"Are we through?" wondered Warren eagerly. "Can we be in the show?"

"You can be in my show anytime," said Muriel. "And if you two bears say one bad thing about the Arty Party Penguins, I shall be so annoyed."

"It doesn't look like the Queen from where we're standing," said Orson.

"It looks like an explosion in a litter bin," said Ursie.

"You've got a bear-faced cheek!" shouted Muriel.

Rory secretly agreed with Orson and Ursie but by now Muriel was officially annoyed and ganging up on her never worked. Anyway, what did he know? Maybe the people who watched Penguin Cam were into modern art and would appreciate what the Arty Party Penguins had to offer.

"And it's a yes from me," he said flatly.

Several duff acts later, Blue, who'd been in her hutch nursing a bruised beak after its pegging, came to see how the auditions were coming along.

"Not great," said Rory, as the rockhopper girls dropped their baton for the tenth time whilst attempting their cheerleading display. "We may have a magician if I can persuade him to come back, the chicks have gone home in tears and I got goosed. It's a disaster."

"Maybe I can change your mind," said a husky voice. "I'm Rock Chick."

A sleek, young rockhopper penguin in designer shades leaped on to the stage with a badminton racquet slung round her neck like a guitar. She was wearing a furry glove on her head which made her look as if she had a funky haircut and it took Blue a while to realise it was Elizabeth, a little rockhopper who was normally very quiet and shy – the transformation was amazing.

"Wow! She's come out of her shell," beamed Rory.

"I play air guitar," said Rock Chick, strumming the racquet she'd borrowed from Waldo's rubbish collection.

Rory's beak fell open in admiration.

"Don't call us, we'll call you," said Muriel before Rock Chick had sung a note. "No one wants to see a scruffy bird prancing about with an old bat."

"I do!" said Rory, a bit too enthusiastically for Blue's liking.

"Let her play," said Orson. "It's only rock and roll but I like it, like it…"

"Yes, we do!" said Ursie.

And as Rock Chick threw shapes and strutted her stuff, Rory and the bears weren't the only ones who thought she'd got talent. Savannah had been hanging about at the zoo after closing time with her friend Chelsea, waiting for her dad to finish work. He'd promised to give them a lift to a party, but as he was still busy cleaning out his fish buckets, he'd told them to go and wait by the penguins.

It was then that Chelsea leaned over the wall and spotted the little rockhopper pretending to play a mean guitar as if she was performing live in concert.

"That penguin is sooo cool!" she said, catching the action on her mobile. "She's like a rock star or something. I'm sooo going to forward this to all our friends."

"I'm so going to text Darren to let everyone watch her on Penguin Cam at his party," agreed Savannah.

After that, Muriel had no choice but to put Rock Chick through and while Rory was really pleased, Blue felt more than a little bit jealous. She told herself not to be so silly, the important thing was to have great acts for the show and there was no denying that Rock Chick was a huge hit with Savannah and her friend.

"Forget Flighty Almighty, I reckon she's the act that will save the zoo!" whooped

Rory. "Don't you just love her, Blue? Don't you feel like jumping up and down for joy?"

"My beak throbs," mumbled Blue.

She watched miserably as Rory raced off to speak to the coolest girl penguin on the block and wishing that she looked half as good in sunglasses, Blue decided that she preferred Elizabeth to Rock Chick any day.

CHAPTER EIGHT

The Show Must Go On

The talent show was tomorrow and the penguins had been busy practising all week. Despite flunking their auditions, Rory had called back Chicks On Ice, hoping that they would get over their shyness and wow the audience. He also decided to give

Alaskadabra a second chance. Although his magic was very basic, it was better than nothing – or was it?

"If I had a rabbit, I could pull it out of a hat," he sighed as Rory went to see how his act was coming along. "But it would have to be a baby rabbit or I won't be able to lift it."

"Could you lift a baby shrew?" said Rory. "There's a nest of them under Paulie's Palace. I'm sure its mother wouldn't mind if you borrowed one."

Alaskadabra thought about it carefully.

"Pulling a shrew out of a hat would go down well, wouldn't it? It's a new twist on an old trick." Then his face fell. "Only I don't have a hat."

If anybody had a hat, it would be Waldo, so Rory went to see the Arty Party Penguins to see if they had something suitable such as a bowler or panama hat that Alaskadabra could borrow.

When he arrived, Waldo was in a filthy mood. It was all the zookeeper's fault apparently. "Philistine!" moaned Waldo. "It's the end of the world as we know it! Art is dead."

It seemed that the zookeeper had mistaken their latest piece of artwork for a pile of rubbish and swept it up while he was cleaning out the enclosure.

"It was a modern classic!" wailed Waldo. "How could he fail to see its genius?"

"Did he sweep up any hats?" asked Rory. "Alaskadabra needs one for his baby shrew."

Waldo stopped ranting, put his flippers on his hips and ran through a mental list of all the hats that had ever blown into the penguin pool.

"Baby shrew?" he said, measuring it in his head. "Then we're looking for a hat the size of an acorn cup or it would fall down over its eyes."

"You don't understand!" laughed Rory.

"An ill-fitting hat is nothing to laugh about," snapped Waldo. "There could be tragic consequences beyond the fashion faux-pas. Unable to see, the shrew might blunder into a crow and be eaten alive."

Rory explained that the shrew was going to be pulled out of the hat, not wear it, but Waldo still didn't get it.

"Have this bobble hat," he said. "But on your head be it if it's too big. If something terrible happens to that infant rodent, I'll never forgive you."

Rory took the hat. In return, he promised to ask the pigeons to look out for interesting things visitors had dropped to replace the items the zookeeper had thrown away.

"We'd be very grateful, dear boy," said

Waldo. "In particular, we need a banana. We want to create a 3D image of a giant dodo and we need it for the beak."

Just then, Clive and Eddie swung by and persuaded Rory to go and watch Rock Chick rehearse – not that he needed much persuading. In fact, he was in such a hurry to get there, he almost overtook Blue who was on her way to the pool.

"Woah! You're keen to watch me rehearse," she said. "I'm glad you're coming, you can tell me where I'm going wrong."

"Ah," said Rory.

"Why have you gone red, Rory?" asked Eddie. "Is it because you're madly in love with Rock Chick like me?"

Rory shook his head and waffled on about a producer's work never being done and said he'd hop along and watch Blue later.

"But not until he's rehearsed the stunt acts with me and Eddie," added Clive firmly.

"Come on, let's go and see Rock Chick. She's beautiful, isn't she, Rory?" said Eddie. Rory gave Blue a feeble grin. "I'll catch you later."

"Whenever. I'll be off then," she said breezily, trying to hide her dismay, but once she'd dived into the water she couldn't concentrate on her synchronised swimming at all.

"Bloop! That's the second time you've forgotten the sequence!" shouted Muriel. "It's front layout, back layout, sailboat into stack lift!"

"Sailboat?" said Blue. "I thought you

said to do flamingo legs."

Muriel folded her flippers crossly.

"Brenda, did I say sailboat or flamingo legs?"

"Fla...ailboat?" blurted Brenda.

"Hatty," continued Muriel wearily, "did I say flamingo or sailboat?"

"Boatmingo!" panicked Hatty.

Muriel pulled a beak-shrivelling face and while Blue was a tough little bird, the combination of Muriel's nastiness, Rock Chick's loveliness and the fact that Rory never showed up to watch her was all too much. By the time rehearsals were over, she was almost in tears and hopped miserably back to her hutch.

She was about to go inside when someone tapped her playfully on the shoulder. She whisked round and tripped clumsily on the ice. It was Rory.

"Just practising a move," she said. "I meant to slip like that."

"Yeah, right," he grinned. "Just as well you're not in my stunt team any more."

To his surprise, Blue stuck out her little barbed tongue at him and ran inside her hutch.

"Hey, Blue, it was just a joke," called Rory. "I've got something really important to say to you."

He must have come to apologise for missing her rehearsal. She waited for a few beats then poked her head out.

"What's this 'oh so important thing' you want to say then?"

She tried to sound as if she didn't care but

Rory noticed a certain tone in her voice –
like she was upset with him for some reason.
He couldn't understand it.

"Well," he said. "You know I don't always
get things right?"

"Right," said Blue, tapping her foot.

"And you know how I trust your judgment as a friend?"

He was trying to say sorry, Blue was sure of it.

"Just spit it out, Rory," she smiled.

"OK, the important thing I wanted to say was, how should I do my head feathers for the show?" He brushed them forward. "Sticky up and messy?"

He licked his flipper and flattened them down. "Or like this?"

Blue stopped smiling and threw up her flippers in despair.

"That's not important!"

"Yes it is. Rock Chick says image is everything."

"So go and ask her how to do your stupid

feathers!" wailed Blue.

Rory was completely baffled by her behaviour but before he could reply, the bears butted in.

"Yoo hoo... Penguins? We've been thinking," called Ursie.

"What now?" groaned Rory.

"Regarding this talent show," said Orson. "There's a problem on the publicity front."

Rory had no idea what he meant and said as much.

"You haven't thought it through," said Ursie. "The show is on tomorrow. You know that, we know that, but how will our potential visitors?"

Annoyingly, the bears had a good point. Right now, people didn't know there was even going to be a show, let alone where or when, which meant they were very unlikely to turn up and there would be no audience.

"What you need is an advertising campaign," said Ursie. "We've thought up a jingle, would you like to hear it?"

The bears grabbed their umbrellas and began to sing and dance in front of the camera.

"See the Penguin Talent Show, on Saturday at five.

Come along to City Zoo and catch it here live.

Magic, stunts and dancing, see the penguins prancing.

Choo choo to City Zoo or they won't survive…"

Rory and Blue stood there speechless.

"What do you think?" said Ursie, who was clearly delighted with it.

"The show starts at two-thirty, not five," said Blue eventually.

"Nothing rhymes with two-thirty," snapped Ursie. "Don't be picky."

"Jingles are great," said Rory hastily. "But there's a problem with the language."

"Nonsense!" said Orson. "We crafted every word."

"It's in Bear Language," explained Blue. "Very few people understand Bear. It'll just sound like a load of grunting."

"Oh, well," said Ursie grumpily. "Take it or leave it."

So they left it and tried to think of a better idea but it wasn't nearly as easy as they'd hoped. If they didn't come up with something soon, they might as well cancel the talent show and the zoo would have to close.

"It might not," said Blue. "There's always Plan B."

"There is no Plan B," said Rory. "Let's stick to Plan A and keep thinking…"

There wasn't a moment to waste.

CHAPTER NINE

Costume Drama

"**W**hat we need is a poster!" announced Rory. "If we put it where people can see it on Penguin Cam, hopefully they'll come and see the show on Saturday."

It was a great idea – the only thing was,

they didn't have a clue how to make one.

"Maybe we should ask the Arty Party Penguins," suggested Blue, trying to put aside her little spat with Rory earlier.

Waldo, Warren and Wesley were only too pleased to help and a creative meeting was held at Hutch 22 where Waldo stashed the rubbish that they used to make their 3D pictures. Despite the zookeeper's clear-out, there was still a lot left including an old instant camera that a wandering Prairie Dog had found buried in the rhinoceros pit.

"It still has film in it," said Waldo, blowing off the sand. "Ready for your close-up, dear boy?"

He pointed the camera at Rory, pressed the button, and with a click and a whirr, Rory's photo popped out of the slot.

Waldo wafted it until the ink was dry.

"We could take pictures of all the contestants!" exclaimed Rory. "That would make a great poster. We'll put Rock Chick at the top of the bill because she's really

popular and looks great and the rest can go underneath – smile for the camera, Blue!"

"Got it in an instant," said Waldo, taking a photo of Blue's less than smiley face. "You'll be wearing costumes, I trust?"

Blue couldn't answer – she was too busy biting her tongue to stop herself exploding at Rory for making Rock Chick the star of the show.

"Oh but you have to have costumes," insisted Waldo, rooting through a box and pulling out a hair scrunchie covered in sequins.

"Synchronised swimmers always wear a headpiece," he said. "Try that for size, dear."

As Blue scrunched her head feathers into a tight little bun that made her eyes squint, Waldo handed Rory a silk tie which had fallen out of a teacher's pocket on a hot day.

"Wear it as a bandana," he said. "Wesley, show him how to knot it, there's an angel... no, not round his neck, round his *head*. We want to dress him, not hang him."

Between them, the Arty Party Penguins sorted out a cloak for Alaskadabra made from the blue silk lining ripped from a lady's jacket and headpieces for Muriel, Hatty and Brenda fashioned from lost hair slides, dolls' knickers and brooches. They made a net tutu for Oo-Chi out of Satsuma bags and with the clever use of scissors and a shoelace, they turned a pair of leather gloves into a waistcoat for Ku-Chi.

"What about Rock Chick?" asked Rory. "She'll need a really special dress – have you got anything in a designer label?"

"Oh, will you get over her!" stamped Blue, unable to contain herself a second longer. "Rock Chick, Rock Chick, Rock Chick! She's not the only penguin in the show, Rory!"

Everyone went quiet. Even Rory looked shocked.

"What is *wrong* with you?" he gasped. "Why have you got it in for Rock Chick? Don't you want this show to go well? You're behaving like Muriel!"

It was the last straw. To be likened to Muriel was more than Blue could bear and with a tortured squeal, she waddled out of Hutch 22 and refused to come back.

"Was that my fault?" said Rory defensively. "Should I go after her when she spoke to me like that? I'm trying to save the zoo here!"

Waldo clutched him by the flipper.

"It's just a hissy fit, dear boy. Best to leave the ladies alone when they're like that. Anyway, we haven't got time. Warren, hop along and take everyone's photo. Rory, you need to come up with words for the poster explaining when the show takes place, etcetera."

"We could use this piece of piping and bend it into letter shapes to make the writing," said Wesley. "And we could use rope, string and lolly sticks."

Suddenly he heard a familiar cough and looked up.

"Cod help me, those bears are always listening in. Can we help you, Orson?"

Ursie was there too, of course. Having had their jingle rejected they were very keen to see how the poster was coming along.

"We've had a thought," said Ursie. "Why don't you cut the letters out of a magazine?" He was waving something at them.

"What's that, a copy of *Bear Weekly?*" called Rory.

"It's similar," said Ursie. "Only the spelling is different… catch!"

Making sure no visitors were around to see him, Ursie threw the magazine to Rory who flicked through it with great interest.

"This is good. It's in Human," he said. "We need more big letters though. Most of the writing is tiny."

Waldo agreed. The bigger the better or the words wouldn't show up on Penguin Cam.

"We'll ask the squirrels to dig out some old newspapers from the bins," said Orson. "Which letters do you need? We can get the monkeys to tear them out for peanuts."

Rory, who was the best at spelling, worked

out what the poster should say:

Talunt Show at Sitty Zoo
also on Pengwin Cam
2.30pm Sataday joon 20
Stunts, swimming, majik and song.

"Orson?" he yelled. "Tell the pigeons we need lots of 'O's and a number two!"

"Speaking of which," said Ursie, nipping behind a tree, "I need a number two. That Mr Whippy ice cream I ate has gone right through me. Shan't be a mo."

It was amazing how quickly the Arty Party Penguins managed to put the poster together once they'd been given the right materials. They had laid it out on a piece of turf directly opposite Penguin Cam and having secured the letters and photos with pebbles so they couldn't blow away, even the bears had to admit it was a triumph.

Talunt show
aT siTy ZOo
also on PENgwin cAm
2.30 pm SATurday JOoN 20
STuNTs, sWiMMinG,
MaJiK anD SoNG.

While Rory had kept Rock Chick at the top of the bill, he'd put Blue's photo almost next to it but sadly, she wasn't there to see it. She had hidden herself away, waiting and hoping that Rory would be the one to come and find her, but he wasn't – it was Big Paulie. She was sitting all alone with her face to the palace wall looking very unloved.

Paulie didn't say a word. He just shuffled over and sat next to her, quietly filing his toenails. Finally, Blue's feelings bubbled over.

"It's Rory," she blurted. "I hate him! I never want to speak to him again."

Paulie stopped filing. "Hate is a very strong word," he murmured. "This is about Rock Chick – am I right?"

Blue was amazed. Paulie had been alone in his hutch for days, how could he know what had been going on? He guessed what she was thinking.

"It's my business to know. I have friends in high places. " He pointed to the sky.

"Let's just say a little birdie told me."

"Did this little birdie tell you Rock Chick was Rory's new best friend?" sighed Blue.

Paulie put a fatherly flipper around her. He'd always had a soft spot for Blue although he rarely showed it.

"Listen to your Uncle Paulie. I've watched you and Rory grow up together. Your friendship is solid. Rock Chick may be Today's Special but tomorrow? Cold turkey!"

"You really think so?" said Blue.

"I know so," said Paulie. "Want my advice, kiddo? It doesn't matter who said what. Best friends should forgive each other in case you lose that best friend to a leopard seal and it's too late to say you're…"

He trailed off and gazed misty-eyed at a rain cloud, deep in thought.

"You fell out with Chubby?" guessed Blue.

"Big time," nodded Paulie. "Over nothing. It was a whale of an argument over a minnow. I caught the next plane out of Antarctica and never even said goodbye."

"I'm sorry," said Blue.

"Sorry? If only I'd said that to Chubby," said Paulie. "*Big* Paulie? Ha! The cap don't fit. I was too big-headed to apologise and now? That chance has gone forever." He put his head on his chest and closed his eyes as if that was the end of the matter but Blue hadn't finished with him.

"You think I should say sorry to Rory

even though he said I was like *Muriel?*"

Paulie opened one eye. "So he's acting like a klutz? This fascination with Rock Chick is temporary. Your friendship with Rory goes back to the nest. Forgive him, Blue. It doesn't matter who started it. Be the bigger penguin and make it up or one day it may be too late, believe me."

Blue was about to thank him for his advice when suddenly he flipped back his head and began to wail.

"I lost my friend, my friend was my world, my world is over."

To her embarrassment, Big Paulie was sucking his flippers like an abandoned chick and looked so small and pathetic, she couldn't keep her beak shut.

"How dare you tell me to be the bigger

penguin! We little penguins are running around like headless chickens trying to save the zoo while you wallow in self-pity. You're not the big, brave friend Chubby knew and loved. Is that any way to honour his memory?"

Paulie, who had never been spoken to like that even by his mother, stood up and gave her a long, hard stare as if he couldn't believe what she had just said. Blue wasn't sure if he was going to kill her or cry. As it turned out, it was neither.

"Whadda you gonna do?" he muttered.

Without another word, he swung round on one foot and walked off towards the sound of the zookeeper's bucket clanging against the rails.

"I know exactly what *I'm* going to do!"

called Blue. "How about you, Paulie?"

But whether he heard or cared, she couldn't tell.

CHAPTER TEN

No Business Like Show Business

Since her talk with Paulie the day before, Blue had been on a mission to make it up with Rory but it had been impossible to get him on his own. First he'd had to speak to Waldo who wanted to know who had swapped the letter 'P' for letter 'F' in the spelling of Arty Party Penguins on the poster; then he'd had to stop Alaskadabra trying to saw himself in half; then he had gone off to practise stunts with Eddie and Clive.

Blue had hung around until darkness fell trying to catch his eye but he was either too busy trying not to fall off his snowboard or he was blanking her. She'd had no choice but to give up and try again the next day. She went back to her nest where she lay awake worrying for most of the night.

The next thing she knew she was woken by a loud rap on her window. It was Muriel.

"Bloop, get up! I know you seriously need more beauty sleep but the show's on in less than an hour. I need you by the pool, pegged, primped and polished... pronto!"

Blue sprang off her nest, grabbed her costume and followed Muriel across the rocks under the fascinated gaze of a coach load of visitors who'd seen the poster on Penguin Cam and had arrived from all over the country to be entertained.

There were penguins dashing about everywhere, desperately putting the finishing touches to their costumes, gathering props and falling over each other to find a free corner to have one last practice out of the public eye.

"This is pandemonium!" heckled Orson gleefully.

"*Penguin*monium!" bellowed Ursie. "We've got a zoo full of punters and no producer! Where's Rory? He couldn't organise a fishing trip in the Aquarium."

Rory was behind Paulie's Palace with Clive and Eddie looking uneasily at the makeshift seesaw they had surprised him with – a plank balanced on a beach ball. It didn't look safe to sit on, let alone jump on from a great height.

Rory had been so busy organising the other contestants, he'd left his team mates to come up with the most daring stunt they could think of for the Grand Finale and now he was seriously regretting it.

"Are you kidding?" he said as Clive explained the act. "You want me to stand on that end and do *what* when Eddie jumps on the other end? Promise to take me to the vets if I don't kill myself!"

"I wonder if you'll see Chubby in heaven?" said Eddie loudly, just as Blue was passing.

She had forgotten her scrunchie and had nipped back home to get it, but when she saw Rory trying to balance on top of the rickety seesaw, her stomach lurched.

"Rory, can we talk?" she pleaded.

"Not now, Blue. I need every second to practise this."

"We're all going to die!" said Eddie cheerfully, bouncing up and down on the other end.

Just then, Alaskadabra shuffled over even more slowly than usual and interrupted.

"Rory, may I have a word, please... in private?" he asked.

"Not a good time, Alaska – is it a matter of life and death?"

Alaskadabra nodded and, reluctantly, Rory hopped off the seesaw and took him to one side. Whispering apologetically in his ear, the magician explained that he wouldn't be able to perform his act as nimbly as he'd hoped as he could no longer move very easily.

"Is something wrong with your feet?" asked Rory. Alaskadabra had been staring at them constantly. Maybe he'd dropped his magic box on his toes.

"There's nothing wrong with them exactly but there is something *on* them," replied Alaskadabra mysteriously.

"It's probably just a wart," said Rory. "Show me."

The shy emperor checked to make sure no visitors were peeking, lifted up his sagging belly and exposed his feet. Rory could see the problem straight away – it was an egg.

"I'm incubating it," he said.

"But you're our opening act," said Rory. "Can't Mrs Alaskadabra do it?"

Mr Alaskadabra shook his head.

"I'm afraid it's my turn," he said. "I can still do the hat trick but the ones where I walk about will have to go in case the egg smashes. If I chip it even slightly, I'll get such a stiff beaking from the missus." He looked so anxious, Rory felt sorry for him. Mrs Alaskadabra could be vicious during the breeding season. In fact, she made Muriel seem like the dove of peace.

"Just do your best," said Rory. "Have you got the baby shrew safe?"

Alaskadabra patted the secret sleeve in his cloak. "He's in the bobble hat."

"Mind you don't trip," said Rory, glancing

up at the zoo clock. "Aghhh… I've got to go, guys. The show opens in ten minutes. I need to get backstage."

As he raced off he went through the acts in his head; Alaskadabra would be followed by Arty Party Penguins, followed by Chicks On Ice and—

"The press have arrived!" called Ursie. "Cooee, Mr Camera Man, over here! I don't know why you're filming penguins when you could be interviewing a handsome brown bear. Did I ever tell you about the time Orson almost married a moose?"

"Don't tell them that story!" growled Orson. "Oh, go on then. They don't speak a word of Bear, right? All they can hear is growly, growly, growl."

More people were arriving – mothers,

fathers, children, grandparents and, right at the front, Savannah with her friends. It looked as if the whole of Year Eight had turned up to watch. Five minutes to go. Rory took a deep breath and counted down.

"Penguins, get into your positions!" he called. "The show's about to start!"

Blue tried one more time to get his attention.

"Rory, I just wanted to say that I'm—"

But he couldn't hear her. He had grabbed the radio that Waldo had given him and turned it up full blast.

"Five... four... three... two... one! On you go, Alaska."

Alaskadabra shuffled gingerly on to the stage to the sound of Radio Jazz, stood awkwardly behind his magic table, produced the bobble hat and felt inside it.

"Nothing in my hat!" he announced. He held it up to the light and gazed in horror at the hole in the wool where the baby shrew had nibbled its way to freedom.

"There was meant to be something in my hat," he said apologetically. "I'm terribly sorry but I think it must have gone back to its mother."

He bent down carefully, hunted around under the velvet tablecloth and in an attempt to catch the egg which had slipped from his foot, he cracked his head on his magic box.

The audience groaned. Rory put his head in his flippers, certain that the magic act was going to be a complete flop, but as Alaskadabra tottered dizzily round the stage, there was a gale of laughter from the audience who seemed to find it even funnier when the magician tripped over his string of hankies, fell on to his back and juggled the egg with his feet.

Waldo, who was waiting to go on next, gave Rory an encouraging squeeze.

"Fabulous opening, they loved him, dear boy! Let's hope they adore our Dodo!"

As Alaska crept off, the Arty Party Penguins waddled on with an assorted collection of rubbish and as the radio Rory was operating got stuck on a rap song, they began to arrange hosepipes, bin liners and bottle tops into a portrait of the famous extinct bird.

"What's it meant to be?" shouted the audience. "Is it a goat? Is it a camel?"

Oh no, thought Rory. *The audience don't get it. I knew they wouldn't get it.*

"Put the wings on!" he gesticulated to Waldo. "The wings!"

"Is it a dragon?" muttered the crowd,

leaning at funny angles to try and make it out. "Is it Pegasus, the winged horse? No, it's a unicorn, how clever!"

And although they'd mistaken the strategically-placed banana for a horn rather than a beak, judging by the applause they were pretty impressed.

The Arty Party Penguins took a bow and left the stage but Waldo wasn't happy.

"A *unicorn?*" he said. "Pegasus? What do I have to do to do a Dodo?"

"Excuthe me, Mithter Arty Farty, it'th our turn!" said Oo-Chi. "Uth ith going to thing a lubberly thong!"

"It's the cheerleaders next," insisted Rory but she'd already grabbed her brother and skated on to the ice.

"Ooh… they are sooo so cute," cooed

Savannah's friends. "You're so lucky to have, like, a penguin keeper for your dad, Savannah."

Oo-Chi did a little curtsey, twiddled her feathers and simpered at the audience.

"My brother will now thing *Twinkle Twinkle Little Thtar!*"

Ku-Chi looked at her aghast.

"No, me thinging *The Penguinth Lullabye!*"

His sister poked him hard in his round little stomach.

"No, no. *Twinkle Thtar!* That'th what Mummy thaid to thing…Go on!"

She poked him even harder this time, the force of which sent him sliding backwards, flippers whirling like windmills as he tried to catch his balance. Spitting feathers, he stomped back into the spotlight, by which time the audience were in stitches.

"I'm doing *Penguinth Lullaby*, tho there!"
And to his mother's everlasting shame,
he began to sing.

"Go to thleep, go to thleep,
There'th a good lickle penguin,
Go to thleep, go to thleep...
Or I'll thlap you with a fith!"

He fell on to his back giggling hysterically while Oo-Chi stamped her foot, cheeping and weeping.

"Thothe aren't the wordth! Mummy? Ku- Chi'th being thilly again!"

It was threatening to turn into a punch-up. Anxious to get the chicks off stage, Rory sent the cheerleaders on and, hiding amongst them, he gathered Oo-Chi and Ku-Chi kicking and screaming and gave them back to their mothers.

"So far, so good," said Orson grudgingly as the gorgeous Rockhopper Girls high-kicked their way through their energetic routine. But he spoke too soon. As the cheerleaders danced off, the next act was hiding in the wings refusing to go on.

It was Rock Chick.

CHAPTER ELEVEN

Hooray for Rory

The audience was getting restless. Savannah's friends in Year Eight seemed particularly fidgety but nothing Rory said or did would persuade Rock Chick to face them.

She had gone all Elizabeth again and

wouldn't speak.

"What's wrong, are you egg bound? Does your costume rub? Help me out here!" panicked Rory. "The teenagers came specially to see you."

She hugged her badminton racquet and refused to look him in the eye. By now, everyone was wondering what had happened to her – especially the bears.

"Maybe she's got laryngitis," muttered Orson.

"Penguinitis, more likely!" said Ursie. "The audience will want their money back!"

Waldo, who had seen it all before, took Rory aside.

"She's got stage fright, dear boy," he said. "It's a case of butterflies in the tummy, only larger. The size of albatrosses, I should imagine."

"But she seems so laid back," said Rory. "So cool."

"Never judge a penguin by its wrapper," sniffed Waldo. "Perhaps you should cut your losses and start the synchronised swimming?"

"We want Rock Chick! We want Rock Chick!" chanted the crowd.

"There again, perhaps not."

There was no escaping it, Rory was going to have to tell the audience the bad news, but to his dismay, they were already leaving. There had been such a long gap in the proceedings, they assumed Rock Chick had been dropped from the bill and as no other acts had come on, they got tired of waiting and began to wander off.

"You're losing them. It's all over," said Orson.

"This can't be happening," thought Rory, trying to stay calm. "It was going so well!"

But the show was falling apart. All the penguins were panicking in the wings. "What are we going to do, Rory? What are we going to do?"

"Pack your bags, find your passports," said Ursie. "The zoo will have to close."

"Over my dead body!" said a booming voice. "And Chubby's!"

Everyone turned and stared. There, standing majestically on a rock in a shaft of sunlight was Big Paulie.

A rumour rippled round the zoo – the show wasn't over! Those who had left drifted back, curious to see what the great emperor penguin was about to do. Paulie waited for the audience to settle, then introduced his act.

"Ladies and Gentlemen. I dedicate this song to the late, great Chubby O' Neil. It's called, *Sorry, My Friend*."

Paulie cleared his throat and began. His voice was sweet and strong and as the heart-breaking lyrics and haunting melody wafted across to the penguin pool where Team Muriel were waiting to start their act, Rory realised there was something he had to say to Blue.

As the song reached its crescendo, Orson and Ursie burst into tears. Grown men were dabbing their eyes and just when everyone thought things couldn't get any better, Paulie held out a flipper and helped a painfully shy little penguin on to the stage.

"I give you... Rock Chick!"

Inspired by Paulie, Rock Chick forgot she was Elizabeth, lost herself in the music and went into a fantastic, head-banging guitar solo of *Sorry, My Friend*. Year Eight threw their hats in the air and went wild.

Big Paulie stayed on the stage and waited until all the whooping and cheering had died down.

"Waldo, what's he doing? Why isn't he coming off?" whispered Rory, anxious not to let things slide again. "I need to take the radio over to Team Muriel now or they'll have no music to swim to."

The Arty Party Penguin stood on tiptoes to get a better view.

"Paulie appears to have adopted the stance of a penguin who's about to make an address."

"He's about to make a speech," translated Wesley.

Big Paulie straightened his kipper tie.

"Thank you all for coming," he said. "But most of all, I wanna thank a certain fairy penguin for showing me who's boss when I was rock bottom. 'Whadda *you* gonna do?' she said. 'If you want to honour Chubby's memory, get off your sorry tail and help us save this zoo.' So for all the penguins, and for Chubby, that's what I'm gonna do. Thank you, Blue!"

All the penguins swivelled round to gaze at the brave little bird in the pink scrunchie who'd dared to speak out so bravely to the boss.

"Oh my cod, Bloop. Everyone's staring at you," said Muriel, preening herself.

"Why aren't they staring at me?"

"Her name is *Blue*," said Rory, as he raced over with the radio. "Blue, I have to speak to you."

"Dot dow, Bloop," said Muriel, speaking through her beak peg. "Id's Show Tibe!"

Blue tweaked the itchy bikini bottoms that Waldo had made for her out of strawberry lolly wrappers and stood between Hatty and Brenda in a neat line.

A hush fell over the audience and to the romantic strains of *Swan Lake*, Team Muriel flipped backwards in perfect unison and sliced through the water with barely a ripple. "By bikidi tob has cub off!" squealed Brenda, clutching at her chest.

"Keeb sbiling!" said Muriel. "Flambingo legs into ballet legs."

The audience was enchanted and as the act came to a climax, they let out a gasp as Hatty and Brenda threw Blue higher than they'd ever done before, and as she landed lightly on Muriel's shoulders, everybody clapped until their hands hurt.

"They love me!" squealed Muriel, blowing kisses to the crowd. "Thank you, people. You look like monkeys, you smell and you can't understand what I'm saying – ha ha – but at least we're squids in, thank you, thank you!"

"Oh Muriel, you should be ashamed of yourself!" laughed Blue, hopping out of the pool. She stood on the side and shook out her scrunchie.

"I'm the one who should be ashamed, Blue," said Rory. He reached over and gently removed her beak peg.

"I didn't see you there," she blushed.

Her bikini bottoms had filled with water and were drooping like a nappy but to Rory, she looked cuter than Rock Chick ever could. She always had.

"And I didn't see you at your rehearsal like I promised," he blabbed, "and I just wanted to say I should have put you right at the top of the bill because you're good for a girl – well, brilliant really – the best – and even if you weren't – which you are – I still would, because you're my best friend, and Rock Chick? She means nothing to me. N.O.T.H.I.N.G.! I was only interested in trying to save the zoo and—"

Blue grabbed him by the beak, twisted her scrunchie round it and bellowed,

"CAN I PLEASE SAY SOMETHING, RORY?"

He nodded sheepishly.

"I'm... sorry too," said Blue.

Rory smiled so broadly he snapped the scrunchie and as it pinged off, Blue fell back on the ice and cackled like a hen. Eventually, Rory pulled her up.

"Coming to watch me do my death-defying stunt, Stinky?"

Blue's heart skipped a beat. "Do you have to do that seesaw thing, Rory?"

"Did you have to do that Paulie thing, Blue?"

She followed in his footsteps over to the rocky place where Clive and Eddie were waiting with their snowboards. The seesaw was nowhere in sight and Blue let out a sigh of relief. They must have seen sense and cut it from the act. Rory snapped on the radio and started to break-dance and because he was so happy that Blue was his friend again, he danced like he'd never danced before – Year Eight were more than impressed.

"That penguin dances better than you, Darren!" said Chelsea.

"That's Rory," said Savannah. "He's always been my favourite."

As Team Rory went into their snowboarding routine, thrilling the audience with immaculate twists and spins, Blue felt herself relax. Their tobogganing was breathtaking and when Rory skidded to a halt by the radio and pressed pause, she started clapping. She thought it was

184

all over but then, out of the corner of her eye, she saw Waldo carrying a familiar-looking beach ball, and there were Wesley and Warren bringing on the plank – the dreaded seesaw was back!

When they'd arranged them to Rory's satisfaction, he turned the music back up and balanced on his snowboard on one end of the plank. Meanwhile, Eddie carried his board all the way to the top of the steep cliff and set it down.

"Oh no," squeaked Blue. "Don't do it, Rory!"

To everybody's shock and excitement, Eddie raced down the ramp at break-neck speed, flew through the air, landed on the other end of the plank and catapulted Rory so high, he disappeared right into the tree

overhanging the bear pit. The crowd cried
out in unison – where had he gone? Had he
got stuck in the branches?

Had he been snatched by an eagle or blown away by the wind? Blue's heart was in her mouth.

She crossed
her flippers and
shut her eyes,
but as a great cheer
 went up she opened
them again and her beak split into a smile.

"Rory!"

He was floating down, holding Orson's

umbrella over his head like a parachute, and with a cheeky wave, he landed safely back on his snowboard and took a bow.

"It's a world first! We've seen a penguin fly!" cheered the crowd. "Bravo!"

"I was robbed!" sulked Flighty Almighty.

All in all, it seemed that everyone in the audience thought the show was worth every penny and later, when the ticket sales had been totted up, there was even better news.

"Takings have trebled!" whooped the zookeeper, spinning Savannah round and round. "The zoo is staying open! My job is safe, Penguin Cam worked!"

"Dad, you sooo owe me that new mobile," she laughed.

The crowds left and as the moon rose the penguins had their own celebrations.

"Three cheers for Rory, hip hip, hooray!" hooted Big Paulie, as Clive and Eddie lifted him triumphantly on to their shoulders and paraded him round the pool.

"And three cheers for Little Blue!" said Rory. "Hip, hip… I can't hear you, Muriel!"

"Oh my cod! I already said hooray earlier – didn't I, Hatty… Brenda?"

But for once Hatty and Brenda didn't answer. They were far too busy cheering.